THROUGHOUT
THE
CENTURIES
FAMOUS INVENTORS & INVENTIONS

THROUGHOUT THE CENTURIES

Famous Inventors and Inventions

Copyright © 2017 by George Owen

THROUGHOUT
THE
CENTURIES

FAMOUS INVENTORS & INVENTIONS

GEORGE OWEN

TABLE OF CONTENTS

INTRODUCTION

There has been just over 2000 years since we started using the AD suffix. Anno Domini, and in almost every century something has been created that has made life better, or at least different.

This book is a gentle trawl through some of the most important, and often bizarre, inventions of mankind, a light-hearted look at the things that have improved lives for people of the time, and often into the future.

Many of us believe that Stephenson's Rocket signalled the beginning of life of the steam engine. In fact, a Roman invention predated it by over 1600 years. Read of how the early centuries following the death of Christ were dominated by inventions from not only the Romans, but also the Chinese.

See how far back in time the classic games of Chess and Backgammon were invented, and discover for how long street lighting has been around.

Learn about the inspiring and ultimately tragic story of a war time hero who is responsible for probably the most significant technological change impacting on our current lives.

And, for those of you staring short sightedly through spectacles, find out about the origins of these useful accessories.

Read on, and enjoy a whistle-stop tour through the inventiveness of mankind over the centuries.

CHAPTER ONE –
THE FIRST CENTURY AD

The Aeolipile – Invented, probably, by Hero of Alexandria

A roar develops, growing from afar but increasing in volume rapidly. You look up, and there above you flashes past a fighter plane. After it, the echo booms. You shake your head at the interruption and go back to the book you were enjoying on this fine summer day.

But what you have just witnessed can trace its roots back a long, long way – in fact, to the first century AD.

Mind you, that dim and unknown past was not as dark as we might think. The Romans were in charge, their Empire was lighting corners of the world (literally, as soon we will see). No, dark days were ahead, we shall peer our way into them in a few chapters' time, but back then, life was civilized. Of a fashion.

The Roman Empire had begun before the birth of Jesus. Indeed, that old scab Pontius Pilot was one of its gentry. By the first century, Caligula was exerting his uncompromising brand of tyranny and the empire was still expanding.

But for all that, conditions were not bad to live in. The Romans' use of sponge sticks for sanitary purposes might not overly appeal, but then, they might not approve of the modern tendency towards toilet paper (a Chinese invention).

But they still had central heating and an organized society. Plus, a pretty ruthless army.

Against this backdrop emerged the aeolipile. Basically, this was a kind of early steam engine. A cauldron of water was lit, and the steam that emerged was channelled up through a couple of pipes and directed on a kind of large globe. This was secured by a thin rod around which it could rotate.

As is easily imagined, as steam is projected on to the globe, it began to spin. Its use was probably as some kind of temple decoration, in which the glory of science could be celebrated. Aeolipiles might also have been rich men's toys, or perhaps just novelties to enjoy in their own right.

An intellectual of the era, Vitruvius, describes using the device to predict the weather, or to 'discover a diving truth lurking in the laws of the heavens', by which we deduce he was talking about the likelihood of rain. It probably wasn't much of a weather forecaster, but then again, with all our satellites and models we still can't get it right today, so we shouldn't laugh at the clever old Romans.

It was probably invented by a Hero of Alexandria, sometimes called Heron (I know which moniker I would prefer) who was a mathematician and engineer from Egypt, then a part of the Roman Empire. Amongst his more practical inventions were an early windmill and the vending machine. Although the array of chocolate bars on offer was a little limited back then. In fact, the machine disgorged a drink of water.

It would be a few years before Stephenson invented his steam powered rocket, the forerunner to the train, but that device can, like the speeding jet. be traced back to works of a first century Roman living in Africa.

Chapter Two –
The Second Century AD

The Seismometer, invented by Zhang Heng

Here's an interesting concept? Did negative numbers exist before they were invented? If we think about it, the whole idea of something being less than nothing is hard to get our head round. However, in the second century, the Chinese Han Dynasty was full of rather intelligent people.

Not only did they invent, create or recognize negative numbers, but they also came up with an idea still used today.

Which practical one wheeled transport tool is owned by just about every householder (note – not flat holder!!!) in the western world?

Yes, the faithful wheelbarrow dates back nearly 2 millennia. The Han Dynasty lasted around 400 years, and as a source of cultural development rivalled even the Romans. Our invention from this period was another finding from this region.

The seismometer – an instrument to measure earthquakes – originates from this era. It was born with a far more enjoyable name than seismometer – it's inventor, Zhang Heng, called it his 'instrument for measuring the seasonal winds and the movements of the Earth'. Catchy, eh?

It was, in the style of the day, an ornate piece. Many golden handles embossed with dragons' faces descend from the urn like structure, which stood at around two metres. At the base were eight open mouthed toads, each sitting under the dragons' heads. The design consisted of bronze balls on the heads, which would open during an earthquake and drop the balls into the toads.

Inside was some kind of pendulum device which would open the mouths when movement was felt.

History from the time indicated that the seismometer worked, sometimes reporting quakes that were not felt by the populations. It is reported that it picked up an Earthquake over 400 miles away, pretty impressive, you have to agree.

The principle of a pendulum moving was continued right up to modern times, later causing scratch marks on a smoked glass panel. The classic modern picture of rapidly undulating lines on a graph is not far away from this.

Zhang Heng (or possibly Chang Heng, we are not too sure as it depends which version of Chinese we read) himself was chief astronomer in the Chinese Emperor's court. He was the man who not only produced a map of the stars and planets, but realized that the moon was not a source of light in itself, merely something that reflected the light of the sun. He is credited with being a fine poet on top of his other achievements.

Classically wrapped in Chinese robes, with an intelligent face and pinned up hair, nobody could doubt this is one clever guy. He is celebrated on a series of Chinese Stamps. During a productive life, he also invented the use of a grid system which he applied to maps. This allowed both positions and distances to be calculated.

CHAPTER THREE –
THE THIRD CENTURY AD

Woodblock Printing, Han Dynasty

Two really significant creations were first invented in the third century AD – both would significantly change the way we live our lives today.

In the Roman Empire, the first turbine was created. But even more importantly, across the continents in Asia, another even more significant invention was about to make headlines. Literally.

The Han Dynasty was, by this time, reaching the end of its long life. But it retained a sting in its tail. Because, it was during this time that woodblock printing was born. This allowed the printing of letters and pictures.

Just think, had this never have been thought of, how would we build our flatpack bookshelves today? (In fact, some of the diagrams for these are so sketchy, they look they were printed on the original Chinese templates – but that is another story.)

We don't really know which individual should take the glory for this finding, although we are certain that it happened during the Han Dynasty. Later, the technique would be used for printing on paper, but in the early days it was used on cloth. Some surviving examples date back to around 220AD.

A couple of hundred years later, the same technique would emerge in Egyptian Society, and even more recently, just 1400 years ago, it would re-emerge back in China, as a part of the Tan Dynasty, which ran from 618-907AD. We are not really sure whether woodblock printing completely disappeared before returning in this era, more likely is that there are few surviving examples from earlier in the millennium, since cloth is not the most durable of materials.

It worked like this: The woodblock was prepared in a relief pattern, with the areas which would later show in white cut away, and the characters which would appear on the cloth or later, paper, were left at the surface level.

It was quite a time-consuming process, especially later on when paper was used for bookmaking, since a new block would need to be carved for every page.

Another complication is that the print would appear in reverse, which meant quite a bit of spatial awareness on the part of the printer. However, once this was overcome, a layer of ink was added and the woodblock pressed onto the surface on which print was intended.

And that was that.

The technique did eventually make its way to Europe, although passage was slower than parcel delivery, just, taking about 1100 years. Here is it was known as woodcut. Some might argue that printing itself is an even older invention, albeit in a way that lacked the flexibility of woodblock printing.

Cylinder seals have been found for rolling onto clay tablets which date back to the Mesopotamian civilization. This means that they pre-date the Chinese invention by 2000 years. But the advantage of woodblock printing was that it could be pressed, stamped or rubbed to get the effect.

CHAPTER FOUR –
THE FOURTH CENTURY AD

Street Lighting (The City of Antioch, founded by Seleukos)

Antioch was one of the great cities of both the Greek and the Roman Empires, a thriving settlement which attracted the rich and the good, the innovative and the important. During its life span, it entertained such various dignitaries as Julius Caesar and Constantine the Great.

At its height, it ranked alongside Rome, Alexandria and Constantinople in terms of importance. Situated in what is now Syria, close to southern Turkey, the city experienced a relatively pleasing climate, which made it a popular resort for the day's tourists. Its dry heat made it a perfect place for the wealthy to vacation when the humidity of other cities grew too high in the summer.

Seleukos, the founder, had chosen a perfect spot. Good water supplies, excellent drainage, bearable climate and close enough to the sea – which lay 18 miles to the West – to offer benefits but far enough to avoid the risk of attack.

Rich orchards and agricultural land was nearby, and the City's proximity to the coast ensured a good supply of fish.

The architecture of the city was a rival to anywhere in the world. With a ready supply of timber from nearby forests and mountains to provide stone building was relatively straightforward.

In fitting with its reputation for holidaying, sports were an important part of the lifestyle, with hunting doubling up as both a recreational sport and a source of food supply.

The city would be filled with jugglers and entertainers, and foodstuffs were readily enjoyed from street markets and sellers.

Antioch was very much the place to go.

By the time it enters our consideration, it had been taken over by the Romans. As a part of the Greek Empire, (Seleukos was a General of Alexander the Great), it had thrived for over 300 years, but then in AD64, as the Seleukos Dynasty faded, the Romans stepped in.

They expanded the city even more, adding temples and enlarging the theatre. Christianity took a hold, and the city became a place of pilgrimage to philosophers and the learned.

It was an extremely tolerant place, a kind of beautiful San Francisco. As well as Christianity, various other religious cults thrived, including those with an oriental bent.

In such a wonderful setting, wouldn't everybody want to enjoy it for as much of the day as possible? Well, the clever Romans came up with a solution. Gas street lights. We are not sure which inventor came up with the final plan, but at the turn of the fourth Century, Antioch became officially the first place in the world where you could party all night, and see what you were doing. (Although, maybe that is not what the Romans wanted.)

During this century, they also came up with the paddle boat, but while these vessels are these days pretty much limited to funfairs and the old Mississippi, street lighting remains a vital part of civilized life.

Antioch eventually fell to a mixture of disease and invasion, but it enjoyed over 200 years of night-time lighting. Even then, it continued as an important city through various invasions until around the 13th Century.

Today, little remains, but the great defensive walls can still be seen snaking up the local mountains – the same ones that provided the stone for so many of the city's architectural wonders.

CHAPTER FIVE –
THE FIFTH CENTURY AD

The City of God, by St Augustine of Hippo

By the Fifth Century AD much of the world is descending into darkness. The great Roman Empires and Chinese dynasties are under threat.

The Roman reign is coming to an end, and various tribal groups are taking control of parts of Europe and North Africa.

Towards the latter part of the previous century, an unremarkable seeming child is born to a Christian mother and pagan father (who would later convert to Christianity). It is Algeria, in North Africa, and the child in question would do little, beyond a petty case of stealing pears, until he reached adulthood.

Even then, he would father a child out of wedlock, something he would record explicitly and with great regret in one of his first works, Confessions, a kind of kiss and tell book of the times, with a Christian bent to it.

Augustine, later St Augustine would, however, become known as one – possible the – most important figures in the Western Church's ancient origins. By the end of the fourth century, he had become Bishop of Hippo, and would hold this position until his death.

He was an educated man, with skills of the rhetoric. He was also a prolific writer, tackling just about every heresy under the sun. Perhaps his early dalliance had a bigger effect on him than we have given credit.

Then, in 410, the world was turned upside down. The Visigoths, a Western branch of the Germanic Goths, sacked and conquered Rome. This pagan people had lived with their more cultured neighbours uncomfortably for many years. Treaties and wars occurred with unhappy regularity. But when the uncultured, heathen, tribe took Rome, shock echoed through the Christian regions.

Christians needed a tonic, a leader to offer them salvation in their times of trouble. The Saint-to-be Augustine provided such leadership. He wrote (alongside Confessions) his greatest work. On the City of God examined the attack on Rome, and considered the relationship between the Pagan and the Christian world.

At a time when Christianity may have died completely, while still a fledgling religion, St Augustine of Hippo ensured that the faith remained, allowing it to become a major force in the world.

Indeed, his work marked a turning point. It was a bridge between the then ancient and primitive religion, and its move into the medieval period. His pragmatism was what early Christians needed when their beliefs were under threat with the fall of Rome.

CHAPTER SIX –
THE SIXTH CENTURY AD

Chess and Backgammon, the latter invented by Buzarjumihr
(sometimes Wuzurgmihr)

By the sixth century AD, the world has fully entered the middle ages. The times we associate with savagery and primitive, tribal existence, though, also saw some creativity.

The breast strap for the horse pretty much completes that animal's attire, adding to the earlier creation of stirrups and saddle. In China, both a giant treatise on Agriculture was written, and toilet paper was invented. We are not in any way suggesting the two are linked.

And two great past time of the world were seen for the first time. Chess and Backgammon.

Chess can be traced back to a game called Chaturanga, which developed in India during the Gupta Empire, although some historians claim it goes back further than this.

The game is very similar to modern chess, with its four armies being infantry, which would eventually become the pawns, cavalry, which became the knights of the modern game, then the bishop of today was represented by the chariotry while the powerful elephant brigades turned into chess's second most effective piece, the rook.

From India, it moved to Persia at the very end of the century, where learning the game became a part of the education for the local nobility.

It was from this period that the terms 'check' and 'check-mate' originated, from the Persian 'Shah', and 'Shah Mat' – 'the king is helpless.'

There is some evidence of board games using dice being played as early as 3000BC. But the first reference to backgammon had to wait until the end of the 6th Century AD, when the game is referenced in Bhartrhari's Vairagyasataka. Probably, like chess, the game had its origins in India, as that nation was fond of a gamble in its early days.

The rules of the game have been found in a book from the reign of King Khosrow the First. For those not so hot on their Persian History, he was the boss from 530-571, and in this book the rules are credited to the triple named Wuzurgmhir, sometimes known as Buzarjumihr and occasionally as Bozorgmehr (why not just Buzz?) The story goes that an Indian King, Dewisarm sends a set of instructions for chess and challenges Khosrow to work it out. He fails, but his minister, Buzz, solves it. He then invents backgammon and the challenge is sent to the Indian King to work out how to play it.

The Indian King fails dismally. Although he wouldn't know it, a millennium and a half later, most of the past time loving world would still be struggling to work out how to play the game.

Chapter Seven –
The Seventh Century AD

Greek Fire, invented by Kallinikos

Although fire as a weapon dates back to the BC period, Greek Fire was a naval weapon of awesome power and destructive potential. The Byzantine Empire was under threat from the spread of Islam out of the Arab world, and was losing ground rapidly.

Kallinikos was an architect, from the town of Heliopolis and his land had been overrun by the Muslim invaders. He fled to the nearest Roman, that is Byzantine, stronghold and told them of his invention. Unsurprisingly, there are Kallinikos sceptics out there, and some scientists think that a team of chemists invented the weapon, with Kallinikos either adapting it or simply passing on the message to his Roman friends.

However, we like to support the little man, so – since nobody knows for sure – we will credit the architect for the creation.

The weapon works as follows: Equal amounts of sulphur, rock salt, thunder stone, pyrites and ashes are pounded together to form a fine powder. This is then mixed with resin and asphalt, in fluid form. Quicklime is added, the concoction becomes combustible.

Warnings from the time indicate that the product was highly unstable, likely to burst into flames in the midday sun.

It is then lit and stored in a copper box, before bellows push it out into the sea, where it drifts, alight, towards enemy ships, setting them on fire.

It became known as sea fire, and for invading fleets must have been a terrifying sight. Ships were made of wood, and therefore highly flammable, and there would be no escape for ships caught in this weapon's fire.

For the Byzantine Empire, it could not have come at a better time. The civilization was already much affected and depleted by wars with the Persians, and the invading marauders from Arabia had met little resistance as they swept all before them.

Then, with Constantinople about to fall to them, suddenly the world changed, and the seas caught fire. The invading Muslims were thoroughly routed and Constantinople survived.

The weapon continued to be used in sea warfare, indeed, four hundred years later the rampaging and pillaging Vikings would be stopped and forced back by Greek Fire as they sought to invade the Mediterranean through the narrow straits between North Africa and southern Spain.

The ingredients and recipe for Greek Fire remained a closely guarded secret. Even as late as the 19th Century an American is alleged to have found a new form of the weapon, and approached the Ottoman Empire to try to sell it.

They wanted its recipe, which the American, who went by the name of Kavafian, refused to yield. He ended up being poisoned, most probably an assassination, and the secret went to the grave with him. If, indeed, there was one.

CHAPTER EIGHT –
THE EIGHTH CENTURY AD

The Vikings Invade Lindisfarne

The Eighth Century was a bit of a barren time for inventions. Up in Scotland, there was an adaptation of the Harp by the Picts. Paper was introduced in regions outside of the Chinese empires, and Roman Numerals started to take a back seat to Arabic numbering.

In South America, a system of recording for example, payments, was introduced called the quipu. But they may have been around, in various forms, for up to 1000 years. This book-keeping took the form of a series of knotted threads held in a wooden frame.

However, little of note otherwise occurred in the world of inventions. Then again, if our definition of what an 'invention' actually might be includes something that changes lives, then the Viking invasion of Lindisfarne, off the North-East Coast of the England, fits the category. It was the forerunner for life in Britain today.

That's because the Vikings would come to change the face and population of this island. Their war like image is not the strict truth. Certainly, the Vikings were known for rapid raids, where they would pillage what they wanted and leave, before they could be overrun by stronger forces. But where they did settle, they brought civilization, education, farming skills, architecture and women's rights to places in which these benefits of society were singularly lacking.

But their very first attack was on the island of Lindisfarne, a Christian retreat loaded with valuable treasures and less expensive monks.

In fact, monasteries and the such like were often targets of the Vikings. Because, attacking places such as these would involve raiding poorly defended but richly filled homes.

However, this chapter is about Lindisfarne. The monastery on this small island, close to the coast and attached, at low tide, by a causeway. It had been a Christian settlement for two hundred years by the time the Vikings decided to pay a visit.

The year was 793, and Holy Island – Lindisfarne – was already in a state of alarm, as was the whole of Northumbria The Anglo-Saxon Chronicles recorded the following entry for the year, from which we can conclude that the weather was not especially good.

'This year came dreadful fore-warnings over the land of the Northumbrians, terrifying the people most woefully; these were immense sheets of light rushing through the air, and whirlwinds, and fiery dragons flying across the firmament.'

It goes on to talk of famine, then the invasion – 'harrowing inroads of heathen men made lamentable havoc in the church of God in Holy-island, by rapine and slaughter.'

Six years earlier, three Danish warships had been spotted in the area, and it was most probably these from which news of Lindisfarne, its location and wealth, were first reported. The Vikings were clever planners, whose escapades were well thought through. It is unlikely that they simply came upon the island, and decided to take a peek.

Life in Northumbria was pretty rough in the latter part of the eighth Century – indeed, the same can probably be safely said for the whole country.

Many religious sorts blamed the Viking invasion, whose violence is reportedly in direct opposition to the peacefulness of the island, saying that it was the revenge of God for the sins of the people.

It would take another couple of hundred years, perhaps more, but this first burst of Viking invasion was the turning point that would take Britain, England in particular, out of the Dark Ages and into a more civilized, more enlightened medieval world, where art, culture, music and exciting ways to kill people could flourish.

So please forgive us if you feel that a Viking invasion is not an invention – you are probably right, but few can deny that to the British in those dark, corrupt times Vikings were something that had never before been encountered, and that the outcomes, after a very tough start, would eventually be to the benefit of the country.

CHAPTER NINE –
THE NINTH CENTURY AD

Gunpowder, China

The Chinese had been aware of the properties of saltpetre for 800 years when they discovered that mixed with certain other chemicals a fine explosion would be created.

But, by the ninth century, the use of gunpowder was reported in texts. A Tao piece with a name that roles off the tongue 'Zhenyuan miaodao yaolue' talks about heating together various items such as sulphur, realgar (a kind of arsenic based sulphur material), saltpetre and, to add a touch of flavour, honey.

The result was a smoky flame, presumably with a sweetish tinge.

In these early days, not enough saltpetre was added to create an explosion, but gunpowder certainly worked as incendiary, albeit a rather smoky one.

During these times, however, we do not think that the Chinese yet used gunpowder for any military use. That would come later, when the quantities of each element were changed. In fact, it would be many more centuries before anybody had the idea, or the practical ability to apply it, of propelling a hard object along a metal tube through their combustible material.

In the early days, gunpowder was used, in a military sense, to power rockets and explode bombs.

It was also attached to arrows, to be used as a weapon. However, use of gunpowder in this form seems to have been largely experimental, because China entered a long period of peacefulness during the couple of centuries following gunpowder's creation.

Ironically, in the early days, gunpowder was known as 'fire medicine'. For a substance that would be responsible for more deaths than we would care to think about, this is a misleadingly innocuous name.

The gunpowder of yesteryear was a smoky substance, and was also known as 'black powder'. Later, it became a smokeless material, which gave it much more practical applications.

CHAPTER TEN –
THE TENTH CENTURY AD

Paper Money, The Tang Dynasty

Money in the form of coins had been around for centuries when the Chinese, under the Tang Dynasty, came up with an idea.

Rather than lugging around all of that weight, why not use a lighter object to pay for your morning latte, or whatever the 10th century equivalent might be? Thus, paper money was invented.

But what is so significant and ground breaking is a notion that we still hold today. It is the idea that an object could represent worth that it did not possess. To explain in more detail, a silver or bronze coin from, say, the Roman Empire period has a net worth – the value of its core material. That intrinsic value is rarely, if ever, realized.

Instead, the coin is used as a representative of its value. Nevertheless, if Claudius IV wanted to melt down his gold coins and hand them over as an ingot of the precious material, he could, and that gold would be worth, well, its weight in gold.

But the Chinese of the 10th century went on a step further. By inventing paper money, they created something that in itself was effectively worthless. It was only the value that the paper represented, in an abstract form, that gave the object buying power.

That's a clever idea, for lots of reasons. Firstly, producing the paper money was much cheaper than producing money from a precious metal.

After all, not only did the mint have to buy the gold, but it then had to work it to make the coin.

It was cheaper to produce paper money, and it also meant that the reserve of precious metals could be kept back for other needs as may arise, such as paying ransoms or trading with foreign countries.

Secondly, the paper money was easily transportable. A pocketful of silver was heavy and awkward to carry around. Paper was light and easily kept in a purse or pocket.

The early form of the money started life as a bill, or guarantee. Thus, a service could be paid for with a paper note, and that note could then be exchanged against other goods, such as food or clothing. So rather than a set value, this emerging money was specifically priced for goods or services purchased.

However, the emergence of paper money brought one of the economic evils of the world – inflation. As it became increasingly common, and began to turn into the specific values of the notes we hold today, so the Chinese printed more and more.

This is called quantitive easing in the modern world, but it leads to inflation. Each piece of paper has a value, but as more of that paper is produced, the amount of goods a not can purchase reduces, because there is more of them around.

Inflation is less of an issue with precious metal money, because a piece of gold is worth, as a minimum, a piece of gold. That is still true today, over

1000 years later. All nations keep a gold reserve, which is literally ingots or blocks of the precious metal. The value of that does change, but is much more stable and universal than the purchasing power of paper money.

Inflation led to a financial crisis in the Chinese Empire, under the Song Dynasty, and paper money was abandoned for several hundreds of years.

Hyper, or extreme, inflation is a terrible thing, making the rich poor in a flash. In Hitler's Germany, during the Second World War, it became so intense that even postage stamps could not be produced quickly enough to keep up.

Philatelists frequently hold Hitler's face on stamps, which are over printed with new values of ridiculous amounts, sometimes millions of marks. Imagine being one of Germany's financial elite, and almost overnight finding your total wealth equalling about the same as a book of postage stamps.

CHAPTER ELEVEN –
THE ELEVENTH CENTURY AD

Movable Type Print, invented by Bi Sheng

Printing has been around for centuries already, but it is a painstaking job. Blocks have to be created to produce text, and each one is a single use object. But the Chinese, inventors of so many of the world's most useful things, are in the middle of the creative Song Dynasty, and inventions are the trend of the time.

Then an artisan, Bi Sheng, has an idea. What if a set of ceramic characters were to be created, which could be moved around in a rack, and print taken from these?

His invention would provide the basis for printing right up until the digital era. Print workers were still laying out sets of letters to produce the day's newspapers until just thirty years or so ago.

Sheng himself was a rather unimportant man, a commoner who was not a part of the Chinese elite. It was somewhere between 1041 and 1048 that he had his big idea. His creation worked as follows:

He would take clay and cut it incredibly thinly, to about the width of the edge of a coin. He would painstakingly add a character to the thinnest side. It must have been work that required the greatest precision and concentration, the thin end of the wedge, so to speak.

He would then bake his pieces of clay until they were rock hard. He created an iron frame into which the pieces of clay would sit. He made printing ink of ashes, resin and wax and covered an iron tray with this.

He would then warm the block of type and press it with a hard board, so the side without the characters would become completely flat. He covered the character sides with the printing ink he had made, and then could print onto a page.

He kept many examples of the same characters, especially the most popular ones, because they would appear many times on the page. Bi Sheng was obviously a highly organized, as well as clever, because he created boxes into which each group of characters could be stored, to make printing easier and setting up the racks quicker.

This form of printing remained in place for 250 years before a Government official, Wang Zhen, realized that the process would be easier to create if wood was used instead of porcelain. 200 more years would follow before the character blocks were made of metal – bronze was the first to be used.

So, as you read your copy of War and Peace, spare a thought for Bi Sheng, without whom you would probably be doing something far more interesting.

CHAPTER TWELVE – THE TWELFTH CENTURY AD

Mariner's Compass, recorded in Zhu Yu's Pingzhou Table Talks, during the Song Dynasty

The Chinese by this point are still leading the planet when it comes to inventions. The Muslim world comes up with the occasional gem, but Europe is many decades behind.

Prior to the invention of the mariner's compass, navigation was by the Sun and the stars. Which made things tricky when it was cloudy.

Discovering the properties of lodestone was crucial to the invention of the compass. Lodestone is a piece of mineral, called magnetite, but what makes it special is that it is naturally magnetized. It is believed that magnetite lies near the surface of the earth, and its metallic lustre attracts lightning. When hit, the stone becomes magnetized.

The Chinese, who else, were the first to discover the properties of this wonder of nature. Way back in the second century BC, they were chronicling the ability of lodestone to attract iron. It was employed as a tool for divination initially. This means it was a kind of device that could be used in rituals that sought to make sense of the world.

These early compasses were very simple in design. A piece of lodestone would be suspended on some kind of frame which allowed it free movement. It would then, because of its magnetic properties, be drawn to the north. Once navigators knew where north was in relation to their own ship's direction, they could plot their own courses.

Although very effective, these early compasses were not very practical to use or move. As could easily be imagined, a heavy swell could have a greater impact on the lodestone's position than the pull of the poles.

But the inventive Chinese of the Song Dynasty soon sorted that. They found out that striking iron pins with lodestone magnetized the pins. These could then be set in a smaller and more portable frame, making the compass not that dissimilar to ones used to day.

The compass is a part of the Four Great Inventions from Chinese history. These are the inventions that the Chinese celebrate as the ones that have made most impact, traditionally, on their culture. They also represent the key ways in which the technological findings have been shared between East and West.

The Four Great Inventions each originated from China before later being employed in the West as well. They are, alongside the compass, paper, gunpowder and printing. They have been adopted by Western cultures as their own, although they originated in China.

For example, the political idealist and founder of Marxism (from which Communism is derived) Karl Marx, claimed the following. That gunpowder was the power to overthrow the ruling classes. The compass was the tool which found new worlds, countries and civilizations and printing allowed the spreading of the socialist word.

He claimed them as belonging to the West. But, as much as a genius as he might have been, he got that one wrong. These were not inventions of Europe, but (like so many others) China.

CHAPTER THIRTEEN –
THE THIRTEENTH CENTURY AD

Spectacles, in which Roger Bacon played a role

It is quite tough to place the invention of the spectacles, although there are some conclusions we can safely see.

They began to be used in the latter part of the thirteenth century, they were probably invented simultaneously (in historical terms, we take that to mean close together) by many different innovators and, they were not invented by the Chinese.

That makes them noteworthy in their own right.

Many historians will place the invention of the spectacles to the northern regions of Italy. Florence has its supporters, as does Pisa. However, the Veneto regions leads the way in the likelihood stakes. There's not much evidence, to be honest, to point one way or another, and only one pair of the said specs has ever been discovered from this far back in Italy, although more have turned up in Germanic regions.

Some historians think it is more about civic pride than historical fact that three Italian cities claim to be the birthplace of the spectacles.

The English Friar Roger Bacon is also associated with the invention of the spectacles. He was living in Paris when he had his big idea and wrote about glasses in the Opus Majus, in around 1266. Unfortunately, not much remains of the original, and this information was taken from an edited version of his manuscripts produced in 1733.

It does cast a slight doubt on the authenticity of claims that Francis brought home the spectacle Bacon.

There is also not any clear evidence that he invented specs, much more exists in his writing that he reported on their need and effectiveness. He had an interest in optics, and his particular religious order, the Franciscans, were known for the practical application of science, so there is some chance that he, or one of his fellow monks, might have been behind the aids to vision.

Nicholas Bullet is said to have bitten the bullet and recognized that vanity has no place when being able to see clearly is involved. He is reported to have used spectacles to help him to see to sign a document. That was in 1282. A couple of years later, there is some evidence that, in the Venetian areas at least, spectacles were more common place than physical discoveries might suggest.

A law is passed which prohibits the use of glass, instead requiring crystal lens, because it seems as though many substandard spectacles are in use. There are further references in Venetian State Decrees of the year 1300 and 1301 to reading lenses.

It may be, though, that in fact we have this completely wrong and spectacles pre-date the 13th century by a couple of hundred years. Discoveries have identified that Northern pillagers and colonists the Vikings with lenses. However, most historians feel that these held a purely decorative place in the Norsemen's culture, and were not employed to make sure that right person had their head chopped off, rather than a mate being the victim of friendly fire in the confusion of battle.

But, despite the claims of the Vikings, the Italians and such like, we are going to end with Francis Bacon. His writings do seem to suggest that he had invented some kind of mounted lens in the form of binoculars. Inventing the spectacles? A true visionary was needed to do that.

But, perhaps the riveted spectacles found in Italy should take precedent and be named as the first true goggle eyes?

We don't know, and our conclusion has to be that we need clearer sight over the invention of the spectacles.

CHAPTER FOURTEEN –
THE FOURTEENTH CENTURY AD

Knitting, invented by many, worn by few
(when it comes to Auntie's Christmas Jumpers)

This is the century where the Chinese finally discovered the benefit (or not, as the case may be) of using their gunpowder for the most destructive of means. Fire lances, fire arrows, rocket launchers, cannons, cannonballs (including explosive ones filled with gunpowder) and mines all seem to be prevail in the 1300s.

But we are not going to dwell on that. Far more important, and peaceful, is to note that this is the century where knitting was first widely used.

Some socks have been found that are believed to date from 11th century Egypt, and there is some evidence of even earlier knitwork from this region dating back to just after the birth of Christ. However, there is a significant likelihood that these were created in a slightly differ way to knitting as we know it today, and used Coptic stitch, which involved the use of nails.

Several paintings also depict the Virgin Mary knitting. However, these are almost certain to be employing artistic licence, as they date from the time when knitting became popular – the fourteenth century.

In these days, it appears as though there was an ad hoc basis to the creation of clothing, as there seemed to be no pattern involved.

Many of the archaeological findings are, as we would expect, not in the greatest condition. In fact, most are fragments which have no obvious purpose – when they were complete, they probably did.

There are some exceptions, such as child's woollen cap which was found in Lubeck, and most probably dates from the century in question.

We don't know who invented knitting. Most likely, it was a craft that developed and changed over a long period of time. But during the 14th century it became a widely employed skill, and was used to make money. It appears on tax lists, and finds have been made all over Europe. In England, where discoveries have also been made in several places, it is thought to have adapted from clothes making techniques brought over by the Vikings.

They weren't just hairy men in horned helmets (actually, that last idea is a complete myth, at least for using in battle – any bash on a horn would reverberate through the helmet rendering the wearer unconscious.) But I digress, back to knitting.

Many of us will have heard grandmothers muttering 'knit one, purl one' under their breath. Indeed, with knitting making a bit of a comeback on the arts and crafts front, we may have even uttered those words ourselves. The 'purl' bit was lost in those early knitting ideas. It was probably used in Egypt, but seems to have been absent in Europe until the 1600s, which reduced the range of garments and goods able to be produced.

Of course, knitting is much more than just a past time, as good a one of those as it is. During the war, knitting the likes of socks for soldiers was seen as a very important activity for those who were in their homelands.

CHAPTER FIFTEEN –
THE FIFTEENTH CENTURY AD

Scottish Whiskey, invented by Christian Monks
or Scottish hill farmers, enjoyed by all

Aqua Vitae – the water of life. This was the name by which the early whiskey was known. Like many foods and drinks, the actual point of its creation is not really clear. Some reports tell of Henry II being served the drink in the twelfth century during a surprise visit to Ireland.

But we do not know if the aqua vitae served then was the same drink. Probably not. But Scotch, or Scottish whiskey was, we are pretty sure, invented in close to its current form in the fourteenth century.

We have three main pieces of information to support this. Firstly, it was well enough known by the end of that century to feature in an order by Exchequer Rolls of Scotland, when Friar John Cor was provided with eight bolls of malt to make aqua vitae. That would be enough for 1500 bottles, a lot even for a Scotsman, indicating that Whiskey was well enough known to be made to order.

However, it was not widely enough in use – officially at least – to be taxed. That would wait until over a century later. Finally, in 1405, we know that a chieftain, Richard Magrenell, died of a 'surfeit of aquae vitae'.

Let's hope he had a good time drinking it.

Its origins are uncertain. It is believed, and certainly the Irish will tell you this, that Scotch is a variation of its own aqua vitae. Scots, unsurprisingly, dispute this. Certainly, Bushmills, which still produces whisky, was the first legal distillery, and that was in Northern Ireland. This dated back to the early 1600s, but as we saw earlier, the Scots were downing glasses of the amber nectar far before then.

When Henry VIII brought about the dissolution of the monasteries in the early to mid-1500s, the monks' whisky making continued, but the people also began to take over production, as supply became limited.

This would suggest that both Christian monks, whom Henry saw as the voice of the Pope in Britain, and Scottish peasants were each producing their own versions of the drink back in the fifteenth century.

The Whisky we drink today is not that far removed from the drink the Scots would consume. Distillation methods have improved, making the drink a much smoother imbibe than would have been the case seven hundred years ago. But beyond that, it is thought that not much was different.

Whisky became popular, though, when a plague of beetles struck the French wine industry. With none of this to drink, people turned to the golden taste.

Today, of course, the whisky industry thrives in Scotland, with numerous breweries producing their own take on the classic drink. So, next time you pour the liquid paradise into your glass, adding a tiny dash of water, or taking it neat, raise a glass to the memory of Richard Magrenell and John Cor, early exponents of the art of distilling, and consuming, the world's finest drink.

CHAPTER SIXTEEN –
THE SIXTEENTH CENTURY AD

The Pocket Watch, by Peter Henlein

Well, what a century was the 16th. It was the century that saw all kinds of inventions as technology advanced. The flushing toilet first carried away the waste of the rich, and both Michelangelo and Da Vinci were at their peak.

It was the century that saw the creative genius of the Bard – William Shakespeare – first reared itself, a far from 'fruitless crown upon (its) head.'

Henry VIII was dispatching wives and the plague killed 80000 in Britain, a quarter of these in London alone.

It was also the century in which hours and minutes began to mean more to people, for it was the time of the creation of the pocket watch. Time keeping devices had been around for a while, but they were giant affairs requiring swinging weights to keep them going. Advances in the technology of the spring meant that a huntsman could check the time to ensure his magnificent lunch was not delayed by an errant fox, and ladies could ensure that their own somewhat smaller feasts were consumed at the appropriate moment.

Although, for those early timepieces, the term 'pocket' is something of a misnomer. 'Dangle round the neck watch' might be a better term, because the micro technology needed to make a watch small enough to pop in a pocket was still a century and a half away. No, these early timekeepers were pendants, shaped like an egg, which could be worn around the neck on a chain.

It was a German, Peter Henlein, who invented the 'shaped like an egg' pendant watch. Henlein saw that a mainspring could work in much the same way as the swinging pendulum weights of clocks, and create something much smaller. However, the term 'much' here is relative, because his first versions were heavy, brass objects, several inches across. They would appeal much more to men, as for many of whom 'bulk' was a condition of life.

However, like a modern wristwatch, their purpose was as much decorative as for the purpose of timekeeping. In fact, they had only an hour hand, meaning that dinner at 6.30pm was a vague ambition rather than a definite date. There was no glass cover on these early devices, although a hinged brass cover would offer some protection to the bulky object. The workings were held together with iron wedges and pins, which accounted for the bulk.

However, by mid-way through the century, the use of screws allowed the shape to flatten, and designs were closer to the modern pocket watch. These were called Nuremberg eggs.

Later on, a trend emerged for watches to be shaped like an object – pieces in the form of books, animals, fruit and insects became popular. It was even possible to have one in the shape of a skull.

These macabre pieces were known as Death's head watches.

Later, in the seventeenth century, men's style changed. The objects became smaller, and pocket watches now were carried in the pocket. However, pendant watches remained the style for woman right up until the last century.

But, enough of these useful items, time to move on.

CHAPTER SEVENTEEN –
THE SEVENTEENTH CENTURY AD

The telescope, invented by Hans Lippershey and developed by others including Galileo Galieli

The seventeenth century was the age of Sir Isaac Newton, a time of science and philosophy as mankind sought to understand its world.

Seeing things more clearly was definitely important in Europe during these times, because the seventeenth century was a time that saw huge technological advances in the development of the telescope.

It was the turn of the century in 1608 that Lippershey saw the light – well, refracted light in any case. The German born Dutchman was a lens maker by trade, and he saw that if a pair of lenses was used, magnification and clarity were possible.

He saw the military advantages for such advice, and patented his invention. A refracting telescope employs one large and one small lens, the larger one doing most of the magnifying.

Later in the century a Scottish mathematician, James Gregory, took the technology a stage further, inventing the first reflecting telescope. This was in 1663, and he described his creation in the publication, Optica Promota. It would feature two mirrors, one parabolic, and the second ellipsoidal.

Rather than being held up to the eye, as per Pirates on their Jolly Rogers, the user would peer downwards into the angled lens. Gregory never actually made this telescope.

Sir Isaac Newton, meanwhile, was improving on Lippershay's design. That had been used by none other than Galileo Galilei, who used the telescope not to spy far off ships and enemy battalions, but instead turned the device upwards to get a better vision of the stars and planets.

The improvements Newton made led the device to become known as a Newtonian telescope, which is a tad harsh on the old Dutch lens maker Lippershey, who, after all, had done most of the work and had the idea in the first place.

Towards the end of the century a further development in telescopic technology took place with the invention of the Cassegrain telescope. In a display of truly European teamwork, of the sort that would, sadly, rarely be witnessed again, a French sculptor called Cassegrain developed a wide angled reflecting telescope that would bear his name.

This made us of a concave mirror for focusing an image and a second mirror for reflecting light. A gap in this mirror allowed the device to be designed in the classic form we associate with this one-eyed aid to sight. The telescope was developed in 1672, although 250 years later an Estonian astronomer and lens maker called Bernard Schmidt would take the design a stage further by altering the lenses and improving the clarity of vision. Unlike Newton, who took the entire glory for his additions to someone else's design, Schmidt was happy to share the fame, albeit as long as he was first named, and the improved telescope became known as a Schmidt-Cassegrain variety.

CHAPTER EIGHTEEN –
THE EIGHTEENTH-CENTURY AD

The Parachute, the first working example
invented by Jean Pierre Blanchard

With this century marking both the first industrial revolution and The Age of Enlightenment, when science was used to explain the world more reliably than religion and philosophy, there is a veritable treasure chest of inventions from which to choose.

Among the many new ideas are several relating to industry; the threshing machine was an idea of Andrew Meikle in 1784, and the power loom came along from Edmund Cartwright a year later. Henry Cort created the steel roller to enable the production of steel and a German, Gervinus, created the circular saw.

The safety lock was invented by Joseph Bramah and Samuel Crompton came up with the spinning mule.

All of those came in the five-year period between 1779 and 1784.

In the latter part of the decade, French dissidents were delighted to learn that they could be despatched quickly via the new piece of technology that was the guillotine.

But we are going to concentrate on something far more important than any of the above. Perhaps not on a global scale, but certainly to anybody high in the air and in a touch of trouble. For the eighteenth century saw the invention of the parachute.

There was a need for the device, because in 1783 the Montgolfier brothers had come up with the idea of a hot air balloon.

With the knowledge that this thought will be spoiled as we delve deeper, the parachute first appeared in the same year as the hot air balloon, as demonstrated by Louis Sebastian. A fact, however, that begs the biggest of questions, is that the first *working* parachute did not come into play for another two years, and was not demonstrated by the said Sebastian. Instead, it was created by Jean Pierre Blanchard.

Leonardo Da Vinci had drawn an early concept of a parachute, but it was a rigid structured device, more of a wing than a parachute, but when Blanchard came up with his idea, his confidence in his own genius was so immense, so unshakeable that he sent a balloon high into the air. And from it, parachute attached, he dropped a dog.

However, in 1793, he had to take matters in his own hands as he was riding in a balloon which exploded. He leapt from the burning bubble and floated gracefully down to earth. At least, that is what he claims – there were no witnesses to the event.

The parachute underwent several changes over the years. For example, the first time it used a harness was after 1887, the year in which Captain Tom Baldwin invented the accessory. Then, in 1890, the idea of folding the parachute in a knapsack was introduced, along with the small breakaway parachute which released the bigger model.

The first jump from an aircraft was in 1911, although both Grant Morron and Captain Albert Berry claim to be the first. One of these, we can be sure, is telling a porky.

CHAPTER NINETEEN –
THE NINETEENTH CENTURY AD

The Cotton Gin, invented by Eli Whitney

This might seem, at first glance, to be a strange choice from a century which saw enormous progress in transport and communications.

It is, of course, the century of the steam engine, but since our planet lies on the precipice of catastrophe through global warming, and mass transport has played at least a part in it (even more if you consider the steam engine in the same general category as the car) we will leave this alone.

It was also the century when the electric light was invented by Thomas Edison, but that runs the risk of too many puns about light bulb moments, and as for Alexander Graham Bell's telephone? Well, if he could have envisaged the sight of people glued to their phones to the exclusion of family, friends, humanity and such like, I hope he would have shelved the idea straight away.

No, the cotton gin might not have been the main invention of the century in purely technological terms, but it led the way for the greatest civil rights movement in the history of the planet.

When cotton became an in-demand product, land owners of the American South needed labour to pick it. As cheaply as possible. Although there were plenty of white people needing jobs, these folks would want to be paid a living wage and would expect some rights.

So, that ruled them out. The answer, to the money grabbing plantation owners, was to find people who would work for almost nothing, and who could be ordered to do as the landowner wished. Because, these people would not be able to do anything else. And, just to make sure everybody knew who they were, they would be of a different ethnicity.

We are, of course, talking about the African slave trade.

When Eli Whitney invented the cotton gin, he created a product that could work twenty times faster than a human. Overnight, he made slavery economically as well as morally wrong.

Naturally, there was much more to slave owning for many than simple economics. Some slaves were treated well, as far as can be understood under the term 'slave'; not all worked in the fields. But the invention marked the beginning of the end.

It would, as we know, take a civil war to hammer the final nail in the coffin of this despicable system, but we have now had a black President. And with the civil rights of the Afro-Caribbean communities in much of the world being stronger than they have ever been – although there is still more that can be done in parts of the globe – this movement towards complete equality can be traced back to the humble cotton gin.

CHAPTER TWENTY –
THE TWENTIETH CENTURY AD

The Computer, invented by Alan Turing, a persecuted war hero

Alan Turing is probably the person who did most to ensure that Europe was freed from the tyranny of Adolf Hitler and his Nazi Party.

The quietly spoken, super intelligent, boy – brought up by family friends with his own parents overseas in India – was written off by his school masters. Turing was interested in science and maths at a time where classics, rugby and a secret liking for cold showers and inedible food where seen as the ideal characteristics of a boy.

Yes, Turing was one of the many forced to endure the British Public School system. When war broke out, this superstar mathematician was brought back from Princeton in the US (the university where Albert Einstein was still a professor) to head up a section of the United Kingdom's secret intelligence code breaking unit, based at Bletchley Park in Buckinghamshire.

Turing was a bit of an odd bod – he had been deeply upset by the sudden death of a close friend while still at school. Telling his fiancé, whom he still wished to marry, that he was gay displayed not the finest of sensibilities to human feelings, but that hardly mattered (or should not have done) when Turing turned the course of the second world war.

Britain was alone, facing defeat to the all-conquering Germans. She was unable to be self-supporting, and desperately needed supplies of just about everything from the US. But there was a problem. The great convoys bringing salvation were being decimated by German U Boats. Interception routes were sent from Germany by secret codes invented using the Enigma machine, a complex and apparently unsolvable code setting machine. The British had an early version, smuggled out of Germany, and knew how it worked, but without the random settings that were used, the machine they had was useless. The U-Boat commanders interpreted these daily codes, set sail, and torpedoed their slow moving victims.

Operators would choose a random word (Turing would discover that they were not as random as the German's believed, and could be predicted) and the day's codes would be set from that. Then, a bit of luck. A ship's captain was captured and failed to throw his code book over the side and into the safety of the sea. The book made its way to Bletchley Park, and on to Turing.

He had created a primitive, mechanical computer called a bombe, designed to decode messages. With the help of this book, and logical guesswork to deduce the word of the day, he was able to decode the Enigma messages.

The British now knew the planned routes of the German U-Boats, and could attack them rather than wait for them to attack. More, they could divert the convoys. Even though success rates suddenly plummeted for the Germans, and losses increased enormously, they never guessed that their codes could be interpreted.

After the war, in both the US and Britain, there was a kind of purge against gay men. Turing was caught a few years after the war's end with a young man. He was arrested, and offered the choice between prison and chemical castration. He chose the latter, and suffered immense medical hardship. He was constantly persecuted by the police, and had all of his security clearances removed, so he could no longer do the work he loved. He died, a young man in his forties, after eating a poisoned apple. No one is sure whether he was assassinated – after all, the British authorities couldn't have a gay man identified as a war hero – it would be the thin end of the wedge. He may have committed suicide, or died accidentally. Most feel that suicide is the most likely option.

Between the war and his death Turing invented the forerunner of the modern computer. It was never made, as he fell out with his bosses and left his post, but undoubtedly the laptops, desktops and supercomputers we rely on today date back to the works of Alan Turing.

But he is a man who should be remembered as much for his work in winning the war for the allies, and for being symbolic of a man persecuted by ignorant and prejudiced British authorities as for his creation, as world changing as that might be.

CHAPTER TWENTY-ONE –
THE TWENTY-FIRST CENTURY AD

Artificial Heart, invented by Abiomed
and inspired by Vladimir Demikhov

And so, we arrive to the present. This century is, at the time of writing, just seventeen years old, but it has still provided its fair share of inventions – bizarre and profound, useful and useless. The hybrid car is doing its bit to save the planet and bolster the profits of car manufacturers across the world.

Flower sound – music playing plants – were invented in Japan. Now that is something that we never knew we needed. Smog eating cement, however, is something that is much necessary, even if it does sound as though it belongs in a science fiction B Movie. Flying wind turbines, that access the winds of the jet stream are a logical development of the land based energy transformers. Agroplast – plastic made from pig's urine defies comment.

But we are going to focus on something from the beginning of the millennium, and an invention that could save many lives. That is, the artificial heart.

The first of these was in fact many years prior to the creation of the object we are studying. Back in 1937, Vladimir Demikhov transplanted the very first artificial heart into a dog. Later, in 1941, Henry Opitek made history when he underwent heart surgery while a heart machine kept him alive. In the 1950s, Willem Kolff kept a dog alive for 90 minutes with a fully automatic artificial heart. Various tests and trials took place, but the problem was that, for humans, survival was extremely temporary, because the body rejected their artificial heart.

Then, in 2001, the AbioCor artificial heart was used. It was extremely lightweight – under a kilogram – and was powered by internal and external batteries.

It is not as reliable as a heart transplant, but not everybody can receive these, and its size makes it unsuitable for about half of the population, but following tests on fifteen patients, it was announced in 2006 that this artificial heart kept people alive for up to two years, after which it would need to be replaced.

Later, the AbioCor II was invented, which fitted most of the population and provided five years of additional life.

CONCLUSION

And so, we reach the end of our journey through time. We hope you have enjoyed it.

Naturally, there are numerous inventions upon which we have not touched. We have looked only briefly in passing at transport, and have simply brushed the surface on warfare and medicine.

We have discovered that most inventions that gained a foothold were developed by others later in their lifespan. In addition, we have seen how many original ideas from the past still play a role in our lives today.

But what of inventions still to come? Will a cure be found for cancer, for Aids and for other devastating diseases? Will man find a way to cure the planet of climate change?

How will technologies develop? And cars? We already have driverless versions, and within the next decade these could become readily available on showroom forecourts. What of those pictures of science fiction from the covers of 1950's magazines? Will we develop the technology to visit far off planets? Will everybody own their own jet packs? Is there a chance of an invention that puts all the mad world leaders who start wars and encourage death and destruction together, in a cage, in a fight to the death, from which the winner takes lifelong childhood as his or her prize?

Finally, how about those other inventions which might just be too farfetched to happen? The teenager who doesn't argue, the washing machine that never floods, the home-made cakes that do not burn? The life that only ends when the subject wants it to.

Who knows? But we can be certain of some fun along the way.